Grease the cake tin.
Cream the butter until soft and white.
Add the honey.
Break in the eggs.
Beat the mixture.
Sift the flour and salt into the mixture.
Warm the milk.
Fold the milk into the mixture for a soft dropping consistency.
Pour the mixture into the prepared cake tin.
Smooth the top.
Place in the preheated oven and bake for 45 minutes.
Remove the honey cake and allow to cool.
Eat.

For Sarah E.M.

Published by Dial Books for Young Readers
A Division of NAL Penguin Inc.
2 Park Avenue · New York, New York 10016

First published in England by Aurum Books for Children
Published simultaneously in Canada
by Fitzhenry & Whiteside Limited, Toronto
Text copyright © 1989 by Elizabeth MacDonald
Pictures copyright © 1989 by Claire Smith
Printed in Italy
First Edition
(e)
1 3 5 7 9 10 8 6 4 2
Library of Congress Cataloging in Publication Data
MacDonald, Elizabeth.
Miss Poppy and the honey cake / Elizabeth MacDonald;
pictures by Claire Smith.
p.   cm.
Summary: A disorganized pig named Miss Poppy
sets out to bake a honey cake, but can only complete
the task with help from her neighbors.
ISBN 0-8037-0578-6
[1. Pigs—Fiction. 2. Animals—Fiction. 3. Baking—Fiction.]
I. Smith, Claire, ill. II. Title.
PZ7.M1465Mi 1989 [E]—dc19 88-3851 CIP AC

Miss Poppy
and the Honey Cake

Elizabeth MacDonald
pictures by Claire Smith

~

DIAL BOOKS FOR YOUNG READERS *New York*

Once there was a plump little pig named Miss Poppy, who lived all by herself in a small cottage in the country.

She was very fond of her food and was always cooking something in her cozy kitchen at the back of the cottage.

One day when she was nice and full after her midday meal, she said to herself, "That was a tasty meal, but wouldn't it be lovely if I had some honey cake to look forward to for my afternoon tea?"

So she took a mixing bowl and a baking tin and reached for the flour to make a honey cake.

But there was only a little flour left in her flour jar!

"That's not enough to make a honey cake," Miss Poppy said to herself.

So she took her basket and her bicycle and set off to see Mr. Rat, who lived at the mill.

"Oh, please, Mr. Rat," she said when she reached the mill at the top of the hill. "I'm almost out of flour and I was so looking forward to some nice honey cake with my afternoon tea. Would you kindly grind me some corn?"

"Why, certainly," said Mr. Rat. "I'm very fond of honey cake myself. But one of these days, Miss Poppy, you'll need something that no one has!" And he ground some corn into flour.

Little Miss Poppy took home the flour and spooned it into the mixing bowl. Then she went to the pantry to find some butter.

But the shelf where she kept it was empty!

"Oh, dearie me," she said to herself. "I can't make honey cake without butter."

So she picked up her basket and cycled down the hill to Mrs. Tabbycat's dairy. "Oh, Mrs. Tabbycat," said Miss Poppy. "I'm making some honey cake for my afternoon tea, and I've run out of butter!"

"There's nothing nicer than fresh honey cake," said Mrs. Tabbycat, "especially when it's made with my very best butter. But one of these days, you'll need something that no one has!" And she put some butter in Miss Poppy's basket.

Miss Poppy went home, cut the butter into tiny pieces, and mashed it into the flour. Then she went to the cupboard for the eggs.

But when she looked in the bowl where she kept the eggs, there was only one left.

"One egg is no good for a really rich honey cake," she said to herself. "I shall have to go and see Miss Red Hen. But what if she doesn't have any?"

"Oh, please, Miss Red Hen," she said when she reached the tiny wooden house where Miss Red Hen lived. "I've only one egg left and I need more to make a good, rich honey cake for my tea this afternoon."

"Here you are, Miss Poppy – I'll give you a half dozen, all freshly laid this morning," said Miss Red Hen, giving her six smooth eggs. "I'm sure the cake will be delicious. But one of these days, you'll need something that no one has!"

When Miss Poppy reached home again, she broke four of the eggs into the mixing bowl.

But when she looked for the honey to mix with the flour and butter and eggs, she couldn't find it anywhere!

"What good is a honey cake without honey?" she said to herself.

Then she remembered that old Mr. Badger liked honey, so she hurried to the wood to see if he could help.

"I hate to bother you, Mr. Badger," she said when she found him dozing outside his home. "I'm right in the middle of making a honey cake. Have you any honey left?"

"No bother, Miss Poppy," said old Mr. Badger. "I can give you some honey. I found a wild bees' nest only this morning. Honey cake, did you say? My, that sounds good! But one of these days, Miss Poppy, you'll need something that no one has!"

Back at the cottage Miss Poppy poured the honey into the mixing bowl with a sigh of relief and stirred everything together.

"Now what else do I need?" she asked herself. "I know! A pinch of salt!" And Miss Poppy stopped.

"Who will have salt?" she wondered out loud.

"Not Mr. Rat, or Mrs. Tabbycat, or Miss Red Hen, or Mr. Badger. Oh, dearie me, there IS something that no one has!" Miss Poppy put down her spoon.

"But what am I thinking?" she cried. "I have salt!"

Miss Poppy ran to the cupboard, found the salt, threw a pinch into the bowl, and stirred everything

around. There was so much mixture that she had to use a second baking tin. Then she popped both tins into the oven.

When the cakes were golden brown, she took them out of the oven and cut one into quarters.

Miss Poppy took the first piece to Mr. Rat, the second piece to Mrs. Tabbycat, the third piece to Miss Red Hen, and the fourth piece to Mr. Badger.

Then she went back to her little cottage, put the other cake on the table, and sat down with a nice cup of tea.

And would you believe it, the honey cake tasted so good that plump little Miss Poppy ate up every last crumb!

Miss Poppy's Very Own
Honey Cake Recipe

6 tablespoons of butter
4 round tablespoons of honey
2 fresh eggs
1 cup of self-rising flour
2 tablespoons of milk
pinch of salt
cake tin 7 inches × 3 inches deep

Preheat oven to 350°F.